CU00833767

TWISTED TALES 2022

TALES OF IMAGINATION

Edited By Sarah Waterhouse

First published in Great Britain in 2022 by:

Young Writers
Remus House
Coltsfoot Drive
Peterborough
PE2 9BF
Telephone: 01733 890066
Website: www.youngwriters.co.uk

Printed and bound in the UK by BookPrintingUK
Website: www.bookprintinguk.com
YB0514F

FOREWORD

Welcome, Reader!

Come into our lair, there's really nothing to
fear. You may have heard bad things about the
villains within these pages, but there's more
to their stories than you might think...

For our latest competition, Twisted Tales, we challenged
secondary school students to write a story in just 100
words that shows us another side to the traditional
storybook villain. We asked them to look beyond the evil
escapades and tell a story that shows a bad guy or girl in
a new light. They were given optional story starters for a
spark of inspiration, and could focus on their motivation,
back story, or even what they get up to in their downtime!

And that's exactly what the authors in this anthology
have done, giving us some unique new insights into
those we usually consider the villain of the piece.
The result is a thrilling and absorbing collection
of stories written in a variety of styles, and it's a
testament to the creativity of these young authors.

Here at Young Writers it's our aim to inspire the
next generation and instill in them a love of creative
writing, and what better way than to see their work
in print? The imagination and skill within these pages
are proof that we might just be achieving that aim!
Congratulations to each of these fantastic authors.

CONTENTS

Mollie Keen (13)	51	Amber Spillane (12)	94
Kaci Chislett (12)	52	Lillie Kohon	95
Lorna Riggs (12)	53	Max Perkins (14)	96
Lilian Wheatley (14)	54	Luana Da Cruz (12)	97
Logan McDonnell (14)	55	Tilly Westcott (12)	98
Joseph Bament (12)	56	Skye Goldsack (14)	99
Mia Gillingham (11)	57	Chloe Calvert (12)	100
Esha Bharadwaj (12)	58	Charlie Cherrett (12)	101
Jessica Mackenzie (14)	59	Harry Owen (12)	102
Lilia Gillingham (11)	60	Phoebe Palmer (12)	103
Amelia Catmull (13)	61	Bella Manton-Kelly (12)	104
Tyler Guite (12)	62	Brooklyn Cliffe (11)	105
Leo White (11)	63	Connor Foy (13)	106
Lauren Wilson (11)	64	Quinn Humphreys (12)	107
Lauren Collinson (12)	65	Scarlett King (12)	108
Lucca Paksoy (11)	66	K Green (14)	109
Mia Koumbas (12)	67	Olivia Martin (13)	110
Jean-Paul Nicholls (13)	68	Alicia Washington (11)	111
Zach Roach (11)	69	Esmé Collins (11)	112
Grace Smith (13)	70	Liam Spiers (12)	113
Daisy Bayley-White (12)	71	Keryn Turner-Dodd (12)	114
William Mbenga (12)	72	Millie Hansford (12)	115
Keira Skinner (11)	73	Tom Craig (12)	116
Summer Card (12)	74	Daniel Hall (12)	117
Georgia Moutray (11)	75	William Rendell (12)	118
Isabelle Preston (12)	76	Kieran Dominey-Patterson (13)	119
Luke Spinks (12)	77	Jorja Spiers (11)	120
D'Angelo Mckenzie-Cook (12)	78	Honey-Mae White (12)	121
Jaydn Hardy (13)	79	Ellie Ashby (12)	122
Bryonie Cliffe (13)	80	Layton Murrell (12)	123
Natasha Daniels (12)	81	Stacey Moore-Nichols (12)	124
Rhys Jenkins (14)	82	Archie Carrigan (12)	125
Alex Sherring (13)	83	Elijah Pestell (11)	126
Ben Habgood (11)	84		
Tayler Rees (13)	85		
Jack Smith (12)	86		
Lucas Bushnell (12)	87		
Jasmin Morris (13)	88		
Olivia Chilcott (12)	89		
William Colegate (12)	90		
Neve Sewell (11)	91		
Emily Hall (13)	92		
Evie Clark (12)	93		

The Littlehampton Academy, Littlehampton

Ocean Melody Jackson (12)	127
Philippa Jordan-Watts (14)	128
Archie Childs	129

Unsworth Academy, Bury

Lucy Marshall (11)	130
Sophie Wood (13)	131
Sam Krelle (13)	132
Barney Williams (12)	133
Charlie Shearn	134
India Wilson (11)	135
Sophie Turrell-Kinsella (13)	136
Ayshe Smith (13)	137
Grace Landsborough (13)	138
Thomas Dawes (12)	139
Elias Spencer (13)	140
Oliver Abouna-Matthews (13)	141
Summer Makin (13)	142
Thomas Dunphy (13)	143
Jake Rosie (13)	144
Leah Wilson (11)	145
Chloé Hill (12)	146
Laila Kirkley (12)	147
Willow Carter (12)	148
Mitchel Massey (13)	149
Brooke Orzel (12)	150
Sebastian Brickles (11)	151
Scarlett Hunter (11)	152
Charlie Howard (12)	153
Dion Senior (14)	154
Will Carter (12)	155
Molly Akturan (13)	156
Jack Corbett (12)	157
Ollie Harris (12)	158
Amy Robinson (12)	159
Amelia Sherratt (12)	160

THE
STORIES

THE TRUE RULER

Winston was the sole descendant of the legendary lineage, Order of Faith. A blessed, cursed family divided by Emperor Claudius in 43 AD as he ferociously conquered Britain. The true rulers of Britain, Order of Faith, were exiled as Claudius birthed his descendants. Winston's sword glistening crimson with blood as it scythed heads that rolled across the floor, blood gushed out of their necks. "Claudius is at fault, not me," sighed Winston. Heart-wrenching screams echoed throughout the halls as a deep voice called out. An arrow cut through the air and impaled Winston's arm.
"I'm Emporer Claudius!" bellowed the voice...

Safwaan Khaled (13)

Abrar Academy, Preston

ORIGIN OF EVIL!

I searched the tomb for the book written by the Devil himself. I'm not evil, let me assure you. I just tried to bring her back. I need to. This book has only been found in verses and brought the two notorious killers. The Night Stalker and the Son of Sam.

The Night Stalker was corrupted by three verses, the Son of Sam turned by two. The only part that was revealed was: 'When the darkening comes, with its darkness it sets'.

I tumbled into another room and a voice came behind. "Stop, child." I've been caught by a saint...

Mohammad Hamza (13)
Abrar Academy, Preston

BETRAYAL

Three, two, one... My missiles shot up into the atmosphere. I looked up at the bullets piercing through the sky. I then faced my beloved enemy. He knew my past. My arms were spindly twigs, my legs were long but thin, and I was tall for my age. I was a poor boy involved with drugs. I was arrested when my parents died. That's when I opened my eyes. Drugs are just powders of despair. I evolved only to have my plan to self-destruct and me rasping for breath. The last I saw was the face of betrayal...

Kawsar Ahmed (15)
Abrar Academy, Preston

THE WICKED PRINCESS

Once upon a time, Snow White was abandoned. In the forest, the king dropped her off because she'd betrayed the queen and tried stealing the queen's spot, almost murdering the queen. She found a little cottage and lied to these seven dwarfs, telling them how she had to run away from her people because the town had no coal for their fires. The dwarfs told her to hide in their cottage while they go fix the commotion. She knew that the queen disguises as an old lady handing out apples. Snow White fed her toxic berries. Her plan was working...

Efe Oto Igbinoba (12)
Flint High School, Flint

REAL BOYS DO DIE

Pinocchio always wanted to be a 'real boy', and because his father would do anything for him, he decided to help him. So, late at night, he would go on a murderous hunt for some little boys. He would drag them to where not even the street lamps could see. He would skin their soft skin, gauge out their glimmering eyes, pluck out their soft hair and, most importantly, stab their blood-pumping heart out. All for his sweet, innocent Pinocchio. If Pinocchio knew, would he be grateful or horrified at the thought of murder?

Macey Bowden (11)
Flint High School, Flint

THE ROLE OF A LIFETIME

Antagonist. Villain. The bad guy. Call me what you wish, it won't change the fact that I have a duty. I was put on this Earth with a role to play and I'll give it my all. He may gain the vote of the people with his flashy costume and obnoxiously overgroomed hair, but it's all a smokescreen. I'm the one slaving away here. Every day I stroke his ego; the world gets to thrive in its pollution another day. I willingly throw away my reputation. The world has it backwards. *I* am their true saviour. He is our demise.

Kacey Wardle (14)
Hall Park Academy, Eastwood

ENEMIES OF THE FALLEN

The raging fire burgeoned never like this. It caused fury within her gaze; his indignation roared, pulsating deep into his veins. *"Enough!"* clamoured Heimdall. Freya halted - only to grin. Heimdall arose. The skies cowered with faces of red, light bent under restraint of his hands. The air trembled, violently directing all to my grand appearance. Silence fell. *Rah!* The ground jolted as a hurricane of electric blue swarmed Freya. Gone. The winds remained, but suddenly a bulge of darkness grew, engulfing all. Heimdall dropped; his energies depleted. He gazed into the abyss tearing his world apart. "What have I done...?"

Nilesh Makan (13)
Hydesville Tower School, Walsall

NEVER A REASON TO KILL

Joy: the only emotion felt by the recovered villain after attempting to redeem himself for his unspeakable acts. "Now I've found you! It's all over now!" the hero valiantly exclaimed, bursting into the villain's abode. Within an instant, the hero's steel claymore burst through the defeated villain's chest, killing him swiftly. The villain hadn't put up a fight, but somehow an overwhelming sensation of guilt overrode the hero's senses. The hero truly believed that slaying the villain for their past mistakes would bring him pride and glory. However, fighting for valiance or justice is never the reason to kill.

Zach Ward (13)
Hydesville Tower School, Walsall

THE REAL VILLAIN

"You lied!" I cried, trying to break the bars that were preventing me from breaking every bone in his body. "So what?" He smirked in the mist of the shadows. "I mean, what could you do? Tell everyone that their beloved hero murdered every other superhero on the planet?" he sarcastically exclaimed while rolling his eyes. But he was right. Who would believe me? In their eyes, he was a selfless hero and a perfect role model, but he was a monster to society, who performed murder to get to the top. "Some secrets are better left untold," he whispered...

Ishika Philip (13)
Hydesville Tower School, Walsall

FRAMED!

Jack was framed. "How could you do this?" Jack cried out in confusion. Hyde looked down on him with incompetence.

"Ha, ha, ha, I have my ways!" exclaimed Hyde. Behind him was a duffel bag full of high-tech equipment. It rustled and clanged together as his arms were getting tired. Eventually, he dropped it on the floor.

"What was that?" said Jack.

"The things *you* stole!" exclaimed Hyde. Jack had a choice. He could go to jail and be locked up for a false crime, or go back home to the city that hated him the most. He was doomed.

Gurdeep Singh (12)

Hydesville Tower School, Walsall

I STILL REMEMBER

I still haven't forgotten what happened last time I was in those dreadful woods. I still remember the gloomy, dark woods with the air so cold that it was making my teeth chatter like a chattering wind-up toy. My heart was pounding out of my chest. I threw a frantic glance over my shoulder, peering at the same tree where that nefarious wolf once was, glowing his blood-red eyes; seeing those knife-like fangs hanging out of his grinning mouth. I still remember me running for my life. I still remember his paws digging into my skin. Then everything went pitch-black...

Davina Bains (13)

Hydesville Tower School, Walsall

DO YOU REALLY THINK I CARE?

That superhero act was all a lie. I didn't care; I never have cared. I never will care.

"Thank you for saving her!"

Gracefully, I accept the praise. Everything I do is an act; the innocent person's outcome doesn't satisfy me, it doesn't appeal to me. There is only one thing that fulfils me. The reward after a long day of hard work. Nothing feels better than that reward. I don't like the job; I like the bonus pay at the end of the month. Your safety doesn't concern me, the money I get for 'protecting' you does.

Amira Helate (15)

Hydesville Tower School, Walsall

LEFT FOR SLAUGHTER

It was my time to escape from the cell that I had been trapped in. The torture that I had endured was finally over. I had stolen the keys to unlock my cell from one of the guards. I snuck past them and stumbled into a chamber, and I felt a cold chill overcome me. I knew that I had walked into Beelzebub's demonic chamber. Beelzebub slowly turned around in a devilish way with his snake staff grasped tightly in his cold-blooded hand. The snake's eyes gleamed blood-red and I knew that I would never see the day again...

Ayesha Khan (14)

Hydesville Tower School, Walsall

THE CLASH OF CRETE

I smell fresh meat.

With that instinctive impulse, I arise from my dormancy and begin pursuit, crushing the bones of my previous feasts underneath my hooves. The mouth-watering aroma guides me through the meandering walls of the murderous maze I call home. And then I see him. A wannabe warrior, armed with only sword and shield, standing between me and my lunch. Wielding my razor-sharp axe in one hand, my clenched fist in the other, I charge towards him at full force, my horns aimed for his feeble chest. Nobody's ever escaped my labyrinth alive. And neither will he.

Jack Lannen (16)
Rushcliffe Spencer Academy, West Bridgford

IS WIND REALLY A VILLAIN?

That superhero act was all a lie. In the beginning, the wind didn't exist. I, Gale, had the ability to control the wind and air. Many people thought that I was a 'villain' with mysterious powers, so one day they sent a 'hero' to come and capture me. She came to my lonely house, let herself in. She didn't come to capture me. She came to kill me. Or did she? She too had a strange power. Her power was to take souls out of beings and discard their empty bodies. Villainy power, right?
I was now the wind. Forever...

Izzy Harris (11)
Rushcliffe Spencer Academy, West Bridgford

A SINNER'S FEAR

My head's spinning. My heart's breaking and my tears are falling. I know I'm dying. I can hear cheers around me full of joy and laughter. Their joy, oh their joy; an emotion I haven't felt in so long it seems alien. My salty tears dripping from my eyes, beginning to hide themselves in the heavy rain. Of course it's raining. I wonder if anyone will be sad when I'm gone. Probably not. I want to get up and wipe my tears, but I'm so tired. I can feel my body slowly giving up. Is this truly the end?

Katie Tucker (14)
Rushcliffe Spencer Academy, West Bridgford

WHO'S THE REAL VILLAIN? - THE PHLEBOTOMISTS

Joseph's my neighbour. The guy next door. Y'know, just ordinary... He lost his job, his husband left him and I was in a position to help. You'd have done the same! Joseph convinced me to employ him. I trusted him. After all, I've known him my whole life. I know who's to blame - do you? "Okay, Vlad, explain how 128 pints of fresh blood went missing in three days from your department. Explain why there's no record of professional qualifications for Joseph. Finally, two coffins were found in empty cabinets *conveniently* in the morgue with your suspected DNA..."

Ash Azam Rajper (15)
The Annex School House, Hextable

I DID IT TO SURVIVE - MOTIVATION

My motivation was survival: I wanted to free myself from killing innocent people. It was a toxic past-time. OMG, I slashed the man's throat! However, I knew it was necessary; it was one step away from freedom. I've killed a lot of people, including family members. Maybe I'm a pscyho?
My thoughts were disturbed by a sudden loud knock at the door. They were here! I grabbed the knife... A case of déjà vu? I've been here too many times before, but this time I couldn't escape. The body slumped, lifeless on my doorstep. At last, it's over...
Restart game!

Cydney Champion (16)
The Annex School House, Hextable

ORIGIN STORY - HOW IT ALL BEGAN

That thing in the corner of his room. What is it? Suddenly, it rushes towards him...

"Argh!" He woke. It was just a dream. He felt dizzy, but went downstairs for breakfast and mumbled, "Morning, Mum." However, before she could answer, he fainted and woke up in hospital. He had huge rings under his eyes and felt weak. His mum had left the room with the doctor. Alone, he looked in the mirror but nothing was there! Scared, he screamed for help, but no one heard. Why? Screaming! His skin felt wet but not with perspiration; he was oozing blood...

Malakai Rose-Matuli (11)
The Annex School House, Hextable

VENOM - WHO'S THE REAL VILLAIN?

Snakes invaded Earth in 2020. Earth fought back and all but two snakes were abolished. They were called Monev and Venom. One was good and one was bad. They sought to protect the world and its citizens. The villainous snake (Monev) caused Venom to kill someone. Monev enjoyed this too much, but why? Monev had infected Venom with pheromones, injecting venom from his tongue. Over time, Monev became traumatised and turned good. Venom was enraged and set out to seek revenge on Monev and the world. But the world fought back once again and both snakes were killed.

Frankie Casey (14)
The Annex School House, Hextable

WHO IS HE? WHO'S THE REAL VILLAIN?

Hero or not; is he really a hero? People discuss this often. They just can't figure it out! He can't figure it out either. They don't like him. He knows that they find him strange. They try to keep away from him. They think that he causes trouble. They sometimes find him rude. He seems to always upset everyone, then he surprises everyone and does something so kind. He seems to create disasters, then swoops in to save the day. Is he that bad or just confused? Maybe he just wanted to be noticed. No one can figure it out...

Joshua Khan (15)
The Annex School House, Hextable

DIRTY SON - ORIGIN STORY

I am 'dirty son'. This is what my mother called me. I am always looked at as unusual. I have no friends, my mom mistreated me and I am only thirteen years old, living in a scrapyard with no shelter, no food, and not one piece of clothing. I am wild, an animal. How could my mother do such a thing? When was I ever disrespectful. All this dirt, eww. It's all over me. What can I do in this situation? Slowly deteriorate in this abandoned junk heap? Then suddenly, I see a helicopter. It's about to land. My escape...!

Doren Walker-Jones (14)
The Annex School House, Hextable

THE JOKER ASKS FOR FORGIVENESS

The Joker and Harley Quinn were relaxing in the Joker's lair when a phone went off. "Who is it?" shrieked the Joker.
"My dad!" exclaimed Harley Quinn. She answered, "Hey, Dad."
"H-hey," he stammered back. The Joker looked over at the phone.
"Batman!" he screamed.
"Who is that?" her dad shouted.
"He is your dad?"
"Y-yes," stammered Harley.
"Ha, ha, that's the Joker, isn't it? You will never date my daughter." He laughed mischievously.
"Please! I will do anything, just let me date her," the Joker cried. "This superhero act is all a lie! Just so I can't date her!"

Charlie Tucker (12)
The Bourne Academy, Bournemouth

TWISTED CINDERELLA

The guests were here. As we know, the evil stepmother and her perfect little princesses were downstairs, chatting on whilst poor Cinderella was washing clothes, locked up in a small room. The house went silent and the door to the little room creaked.

"Um, ma'am?" Stepmother mumbled. "The guests are gone."

Cinderella looked up. "Finally. Why are you still standing there? Get to work! Along with your ugly daughters."

"Yes, miss," Stepmother answered. Cinderella sighed and sat down on her sparkling golden throne.

"Why? Just why?" Stepmother asked.

"What, do you think people will believe you?" Cinderella laughed loudly.

Sarah Gasparovic (12)
The Bourne Academy, Bournemouth

THE TRUE ORIGIN OF STRUCKSTONE

"This is BBC News. The villain Struckstone has been cornered by police and Krypton."

"Commissioner Gordan, sir, it's time. I'll tell you *my* origins, not my fake brother's ones..."

It was a nice day twenty years ago. "Bro, catch." *Whoosh!*

"Hey! That could have hit me. Wait, *nooo!* You broke my lab window and hit Lazo!"

I went to make sure that my robot was okay. "It's fin-"

Bang! I almost died because of him. That's my origin.

Present: "Oh my... Krypton, how dare you! Wait..." Krypton went past him. It was on purpose. "Arrest Krypton, men!"

TeeJay Chiddi (11)
The Bourne Academy, Bournemouth

A CHANGE FOR THE WORST

"I have done it."

"Have you?"

"It was all a lie. I now have enough evidence to frame the president."

"How? What are your powers?"

"By using the quantum dynamics alternate universe, I can change my appearance."

"What? *Nooo!*"

"You can't stop it. It's all over."

"How do I stop it?"

"You can't, Boston."

"I'll get you one day, Ninez. Even if I die for it," he said in his last moments. Little did Ninez know, when the universes collided, it left an explosion. Ten trillion times hotter than the sun. Nothing remained.

Luke Wilson (11)
The Bourne Academy, Bournemouth

NOT EVERYONE GETS A CAPE

It was a dirty atmosphere.

"Why'd you take this path?" questioned the interrogator.

Joker stuttered while whispering, "It wasn't my fault, they made me..."

"Why'd you kill them?" argued the interrogator.

"They made fun of my voice, my style, my everything. They did it!" screamed Joker. "They put this on me, I couldn't take it," sighed Joker.

"You are a crazy, unstable, misleading creature!" shouted the man.

"*No I'm not!*" yelled Joker, getting out of the chair and pinning the man to the wall. "No, I am not," wept Joker, faintly smiling.

Nash Afram (12)
The Bourne Academy, Bournemouth

PLANKTON THE KILLER

"Hey, look!" shouted Mr. Krabs. "What is Plankton doing?"
"I don't know," replied SpongeBob.
"It looks like he's coming our way. Let's say hi," Mr. Krabs suggested.
"Sure," SpongeBob agreed. And just as he said that, Plankton took out a knife and slashed SpongeBob across his square pants, killing him! In horror, Mr. Krabs yelled and gasped. Running as fast as his little legs could go, he yelled for help. Suddenly, the whole village was Planktons. Strangely, Plankton's eyes turned red as he evolved into Mega Plankton with a mission to take over the entire world! He had won (temporarily)...!

Samuel Chilcott (12)

The Bourne Academy, Bournemouth

AM I THE REAL VILLAIN?

It was a gloomy night. The sky was ominous and mist covered the forest like a veil. I was counting cash that I'd recently 'borrowed' from the nearby bank when, all of a sudden, my hideout exploded in a shower of bricks. "Oh, it's you again," I said, scowling at the hero. She just frowned. "Come, you're going to prison."
I clenched my fists. "I'm not leaving without paying my brother's ransom."
"Oh, your brother..." the hero said with a malicious cackle. "You'll never see him again. See, I've had him all along. But nobody will believe you, pathetic criminal!"

Katie Assad (11)
The Bourne Academy, Bournemouth

FRAMED

It was another day relaxing by a warm open fire. I watched in disgust, my arch-nemesis fighting crime on the TV. "Stupid heroes," I muttered to myself. As I slowly got up to brew another coffee on my day off from mischievous plotting, Tracer burst through the door.

"Reaper!" she exclaimed.

"Ugh, what do you want?" I said miserably.

"I know it was you who robbed that bank on North Street! Admit!" she shouted.

"What? I've been here all day!" I bickered.

"Oh really?" she said smugly and held up photos of an imposter. "Who will they believe, Reaper?"

Josh Marshall (14)
The Bourne Academy, Bournemouth

FEEL MY WRATH

I never really belonged here. I was always killing animals for entertainment. I think I'm a psychopath. Lightning Strike, my enemy, looked weak. I smiled. Strike looked at me and said, "Wrath, I feel like you are a misunderstood girl. It's okay if you have trauma, I'll understand, I'm-"
I grabbed her throat, my anger rising. Strike gasped for air, then suddenly stopped. My eye twitched. She was dead. I'd killed Lightning Strike. I suddenly felt like I wasn't a psychopath anymore. Emotions flooded me. I wasn't a cold-blooded, heartless villain. Lightning Strike was right; I was a misunderstood girl.

Lyla Hartnell (14)
The Bourne Academy, Bournemouth

THE 'VILLAIN' AND THE 'HERO'

His sword cut straight through the villain who fell to his knees and mumbled, "I will come back." He dropped to the floor. He was dead. Finally. Our hero strode towards the exit and - ugh, who am I fooling? This is how it actually goes... Our 'villain' falls to his knees. "No one will believe you're the hero..." and drop. The 'villain' is dead. Slowly walking to the exit, our 'hero' laughs. Opening the door, millions of people flood in, asking questions about the battle.

"Is the villain dead?" asks a news reporter.

"Yes, yes he is," smiles the 'hero'.

Enya Weir (13)
The Bourne Academy, Bournemouth

MR MC'STRAWBERRY

Peter Rabbit and his friends stole all of Mr McGregor's strawberries. They thought that they were sneaky, but that same day, 1 o'clock in the afternoon, Mr McGregor noticed that his strawberries were gone. "Darn rabbits, I'll get you one day!" he shrieked as he paced around his garden, wondering what he could do to stop them. Then came a shout that slowly turned into silence.

"What happened?" questioned Peter. He hopped into Mr McGregor's garden. He had turned into a strawberry! Peter thought, *yes, I have defeated the witch!* but soon he'd have to realise that ain't the case...

Emilia Davis (12)
The Bourne Academy, Bournemouth

MALEFICENT'S CONCERN

Maleficent lurked within her dark fortress. She hid from outsiders who had no place within her forest of devilish destruction. The ravens around her throne began to worry, knowing that something was bothering their beloved mistress. Maleficent's thoughts consumed her mind, keeping her hostage in a mess of her mistakes. Was there something in particular that trapped her within this miserable misfortune? 'Twas Princess Aurora. Why? I hear you ask. Why should the princess concern the 'Mistress of All Evil'? She couldn't bear to push the girl out of her head. For the darling Aurora was the dark queen's daughter...

Bethany Davies (12)
The Bourne Academy, Bournemouth

BATMAN AND ROBIN - GOOD OR EVIL?

It was dinnertime in the Joker's home. His three young children were eating their meals, happily spending quality time with their beloved father. It was rare that they could do this. Although their dad was innocent, he was always framed for Batman and Robin's terrible deeds. There was a knock at the door. Silence... Suddenly, the door was blasted open. Batman and Robin stood, cackling in the dust.
"We've come to frame you, Joker!" Robin exclaimed.
"Why? What did I do?" Joker asked, comforting the children.
"You robbed someone, now come to prison!" Batman cried...

Ruby Herbert (12)
The Bourne Academy, Bournemouth

GRANNY'S FRIEND WOLF

In the woods, Wolf was starving when he got a letter.
'Please eat me!' It was a miracle. Wolf went to the address
and the door was open.
"Help me, I'm in so much pain, just finish me off!" cried
Granny.
"I'll be despised for this."
"No, you won't. I've written a letter explaining everything."
"I guess it's a win-win situation because I won't be hungry
and you won't be in any more pain." Wolf grabbed her
without another thought. Apart from being a bit bony, it
was the best meal he'd had in what felt like forever.

Jacob Lotriet (12)
The Bourne Academy, Bournemouth

SIMBA BETRAYS THE PRIDE LANDS: SCAR'S END

It was a lovely day in the Pride Lands until Simba's trusty friend saw Nala, Simba's wife, dead, murdered. He heard the news and he suspected one person: Scar. Scar is Simba's evil uncle who murdered Mufasa, Simba's father.

Simba runs to find Scar. He finally finds Scar and confronts him. Scar denies it, but Simba does not believe him. Scar sees some blood on Simba's teeth and he says, "You're framing me? But why?"

"Yeah, I am framing you! Who will they believe? You, Scar, or me, Simba, the king?"

Scar says, "Why would you do this, Simba?"

Harry Holburn (12)

The Bourne Academy, Bournemouth

THE VOICES

Beep! As usual, the steel door slid open. Three... two...
"We need you!" called out an unfamiliar voice. I was
shocked. No one ever asked me for help; maybe this was the
start. I sprang up from my seat and slipped on the
mandatory chem suit.
"It's a yes... then follow me," he said. Before I knew it, we
arrived at the undisclosed location. I was handed a rifle.
Suddenly, a shriek pierced the thick vegetation, muzzle
flashes lit up the twelve-foot monster. I took aim, time
slowed. I pulled the trigger, then *thump...!* I awake to the
usual beeping.

Miguel Marques (12)
The Bourne Academy, Bournemouth

CLETUS

Crash! The Citadel was completely destroyed, including Venom and Eddie. Cletus began to cackle. "I've done it! I've finally done it..." He slumped down against the bricks and began to reminisce on his past. Right from childhood, he had always been abnormal. He would be consistently bullied and teased to the point where he'd had enough. Instead of feeling fear, he wanted others to fear him. And he was feared, especially now. Ever since Carnage took over his body, his life had been turned upside down. In a negative way. After all this, could he still redeem himself?

Nancy Roche (12)
The Bourne Academy, Bournemouth

THE TRUTH BEHIND WONDER WOMAN

Everyone thinks that I'm a hero. Everyone thinks that I save people. That superhero act's all a lie. They don't know the real me. I don't save people because I like to help. I save people for money and fame. Framing people is my speciality!

"I know the truth!" Dad shouts.

"What do you mean?" I question him.

"I know you frame people just to save them for fame!" he yells.

"Well, you know now," I tell him. "If you tell them, who will they believe, me or you?" I cackle. I gain their trust; it's easy to frame them.

Amaiya Tomey (12)
The Bourne Academy, Bournemouth

THE BAD WOLF

When Little Red Riding Hood 'saved' her grandma, she tied her to a rusty chair. Grandma said, "What are you doing?" Little Red Riding Hood said, "You know why we're here... Why didn't you tell me you adopted me? I hate you!" Grandma said, "I'm sorry, darling, really sorry!" When the wolf turned up, all the pigs stood outside.

"Don't worry, Grandma, I'll save you, I promise!" Then Little Red Riding Hood said, "What? No!" Out of the blue, the wolf said, "Yeah, I just pretended to be the bad guy."

Lucas Franklin-Andrews (12)
The Bourne Academy, Bournemouth

VICTORIOUS VILLAIN, OR SO HE THOUGHT

"For my final wish, I want all the riches in the world."
"Your wish is my command."
The sky turned grey. Everything stopped. Instead of revolving around the sun, it revolved around me. Walking home, people were on the streets. Some sitting, some crying, but one in particular caught my eye. A girl, no older than seven, looked at her mum and said, "When can we go home?" It got to me. I went back to the genie and cried, "Take it all back please."
"Can't take back wishes."
I lived in guilt for the rest of my life.

Sienna Comaskey (11)
The Bourne Academy, Bournemouth

BACK IN BUSINESS

He sat on top of the burning building, stuck. The Herdes Tower was up in flames. He was still, wondering which villain could have caused this. The Jester? No, he died two years ago. How? Nobody knows. A smile painted his bruised face. That smile faded into a sinister grin. He approached the ledge and yells filled the atmosphere. They instantly recognised him. "Back in business!" he laughed, jumping off the ledge and fading away with a loud echoing bang! Panic arose and the heroes were in shock. The Jester just smiled. He wasn't dead. The heroes could only dream...

Evie Saunders (12)
The Bourne Academy, Bournemouth

THE CHURCHES' BURDEN

Her cold, dead hands squeezing my scarred arm, pale eyes faded of life, her black lungs gasped for the unclean air that filled the room. "Why, Father?" she cried. I chose to ignore her and reached for another handful of painkillers. "What path have I gone down, my Lord?" I lay her to rest.
"Jesus, who tends the shepherd, bless this little lamb tonight through the darkness until morning's delight." I prayed for her. I took another hit of painkillers to calm me as the prince of darkness sealed my fate. God may send my soul down to Hell...

Jack Steyn (13)
The Bourne Academy, Bournemouth

44

DREADED DEMON

Since I was born, I was treated like, looked at and have always been an outsider. When *she* was born, it changed. Natsu was different to others. She was smart and beautiful. Natsu instantly got accepted by the community and got treated like a goddess until they found her birthplace. An execution was arranged, to burn her to death. By the time I found out, it was too late. She lay on the ground, covered in black marks. Suddenly, *he* appeared...

"It seems you need my aid," the figure cackled. "But you need to promise me something..."

Lukas Custodio (13)

The Bourne Academy, Bournemouth

THE CANCER PIRATE

Oman Shink, a geography teacher diagnosed with lung cancer on a low income, came up with the idea to become a pirate after hearing of the profits it could bring his family. He recruited trustworthy people to join his crew. He rummaged through his family's old things to find a speedboat that they could use. When they met, Oman's geography knowledge helped them to find the perfect place to hit the ships. They successfully hit them several times, but they got wise and something terrible happened to Oman, and it turned out that one of them wasn't so trustworthy...

Harrison Lamb (13)
The Bourne Academy, Bournemouth

VADER'S CONTEMPLATION

Darth Vader - the Dark Lord of the Sith - boarded his triangular shuttle and arrived at the screeching Star Destroyer. Exiting the shuttle to five rows of 100 white helmets, Vader traversed the Star Destroyer until he reached his chamber. Vader sat in his bacta tank and fell asleep. Anakin started to receive flashbacks of the fight on Mustafar, when he was burned alive and his wife died in childbirth. A thought of four words raced through his head: *should I kill him?* His thoughts of his master were simple, full of hatred. *I should, for her, for Padme...*

Ashton Berndt (13)
The Bourne Academy, Bournemouth

ONE TOUCH AND VENOM TAKES CONTROL!

Venom is a symbiote that has evolved into a creature that can control people. Although, he sometimes loses control of himself and turns into a violent, ferocious creature. When Venom gets angry, he is an unstoppable machine! He can use his alien enormous body to jump from building to building in only seconds. If people saw Venom, they'd all freeze like ice cubes, in fear. The police have tried to capture him many times, but he's still roaming the world. He has caused much damage. People are terrified of this insane strong monster that needs to be stopped now!

Batu Sali (12)
The Bourne Academy, Bournemouth

THE REDEMPTION OF THE BIG BAD WOLF

It all started last month. I thought to myself, *why am I always thought of as a villain?* I had a great idea. I should build the helpless pigs new houses as I blew down all their old ones. I got to work. I even supplied my own bricks. I would never steal anything again. Jimmy, Johnny and James - the three pigs - were astounded by the idea.

Five weeks later, I had finished all three houses.

"How much do we owe you?" yelled Johnny.

"Nothing!" I shouted back. "Let's now forget all about our past!" And so we did.

Harley Guy (12)
The Bourne Academy, Bournemouth

OPERATION BANG!

I'm enjoying this day off from beating up Batman. A tropical island is a great place for hatching plans to kill him though. Taking a break from villainy feels really good, but I despise Batman. I want to blow him up for good! He'll be the big joke that will go down with a big bang! Ha, ha! Wait... What's the plan? I'll trap him in a building, put bombs around it - then... *kaboom!* It's going to be bangtastic! Ha, ha! What an amazing plan. Tomorrow night, Batman - you'll be no more. This is it - 'Operation Bang'. Ha, ha, ha!

Levi Mortimer-West (13)
The Bourne Academy, Bournemouth

THE FEAR OF SOMEONE FINDING OUT!

My newest victim: a girl aged fourteen, her name is Katy. She knew she was bisexual for a while, but never wanted to admit it for fear of me! Coming Out; I'm the fear no gay person wants to face but has to. Today she has plucked up the courage to overcome me.

Scaredly knocking on her mum's door, she entered and mumbled, "Mum, I... I'm gay," Without questioning, her mum ran over and held her in a tight, comforting bear hug. No! She's done it, she's overcome me! Luckily, I have many more victims to torment for years coming.

Mollie Keen (13)

The Bourne Academy, Bournemouth

THE BULLY

I never really belonged here. I saw the girl at the cafeteria, getting her food. "Hey!"
"Um, hi." I pushed her over, knocking her food out of her hands, everyone taking pictures. Not wanting to go home, I walked slowly, taking ten minutes longer than usual. Before I even got to the door, I heard my parents arguing. I sat on the doorstep and sobbed. Watching my dad leave, I looked at my mum. Without looking back, I ran. As I ran away, I stopped when trees twisted in my mind, the pavement caved in. I don't want this anymore...

Kaci Chislett (12)
The Bourne Academy, Bournemouth

THE OVERFLOW

When God created the Earth, he made everyone, everything and every animal immortal. They never died. So, in order to stop the overflow of living things, God created death and the Grim Reaper. He was in charge of reaping every dead soul. The reason God had to make death was because nobody could die and the overflow was getting on everyone's nerves. Fights were starting to break out. If God did not do something soon, a whole war would break out. When Death came strolling along, people were relieved. At the time, it was a blessing. Now it's a fear!

Lorna Riggs (12)
The Bourne Academy, Bournemouth

BURNING DOWN IN HELL

Lucifer. That's my name. Though it may be abbreviated to fit the subject of misunderstanding. I once was angelic; popular amongst the heavens. And with wings of cotton. I wondered. *Only one thing gets on my nerves. God.*
I confront him. "Why are you so powerful?" I ask, now with regret as I recall a mere second later my wings smouldered to ash. And I am chained to the core of the Earth for all of eternity. Through the doors to the depths of Hell; the doors that bind and block all hopelessness. But I will escape. I am Lucifer.

Lilian Wheatley (14)
The Bourne Academy, Bournemouth

THE FIEND

It is complete. He is complete. The plan was a success. This thing is powerful enough to destroy them. A maniacal screech echoed in the room. Yes, we are ready, our plan to destroy the United Kingdom is ago. But wait; life isn't that simple. People say I'm crazy. But I'm not! No, I'm far from crazy. The lever to the cage crawled upwards. The fiendish character sprawled out of the cage. It stood up, stopped. Stared. Waited. He was as horrific as a ghoul. Almost as though he was dead. Lord have mercy on this country as they're doomed!

Logan McDonnell (14)
The Bourne Academy, Bournemouth

WHO'S WHO?

Finally, I've got my day off from the job.

It was a horrible day that day. But I will tell you how it all went down. So I was chillin' on my swivel chair and then *boom!* My door blew down to the floor. Then the supposed 'hero' walked inside.

"Well, well, well. Who do we have here?" said the evil hero. I was shocked and I got up and ran off. But that wasn't enough. She jumped in front of me and said, "You're coming with me, boy!" Then I could tell that she isn't nice, she's evil...

Joseph Bament (12)
The Bourne Academy, Bournemouth

WOLF CHANGES HEART

As Little Red Riding Hood was skipping to her nan's house, she was listening to the birds sing. She went into her nan's house and suddenly saw the grey wolf pouring the nan tea. Little Red Riding Hood was surprised and asked the wolf, "Why are you here, Wolf?"

The wolf replied, "I have to make up for what I have done. I'm so sorry."

Little Red Riding Hood cuddled the wolf and he replied, "Thank you." They went to the field and sat down, having a tea party. The wolf's heart had changed forever.

Mia Gillingham (11)

The Bourne Academy, Bournemouth

IT WASN'T ME?

When I switched on the TV, turning on the news, I didn't expect my name plastered over the screen! What? I watched on further, I had apparently... broken into a building? Stole valuable items? I was certain that I had never done that. Suddenly, there was a knock on my door. The police? Was I going to get arrested? The door broke down and what I saw was the police... and my best friend? The police immediately searched the place. My best friend leaned over to me. "Enjoy going to jail for the crime I committed," she whispered. I gasped.

Esha Bharadwaj (12)
The Bourne Academy, Bournemouth

THE BIRTH OF MOTHER GOTHEL

It started in a delicate town nestled in the sorcerer's forest. A lady (to be precise Mariana Gothel) crouched in a worn, tattered armchair, mourning her sweet beloved. Hopelessly, she stared at her immaculate garden that her husband had shed blood and sweat on. Mariana missed him dearly and vowed to keep the garden the way it was, in memory of him. Suddenly, a loud snap was heard and Mariana jumped out of her chair like a jack-in-the-box. Racing outside, she pounced on a small girl reaching for an apple. This was the birth of Mother Gothel.

Jessica Mackenzie (14)
The Bourne Academy, Bournemouth

HARLEY QUINN'S SORROW

As I walked onto the stage, I quoted, "I have to make up for what I've done. I'm sorry for what I've done and I don't know how to make it up to you. I know I never belonged, so I will leave." As I walked to the back of the stage, I heard in the distance, "What? Why?" Suddenly, the clapping started. I walked out, saw the crowd, then they cheered. In my head I heard, *thank you*, but my gut said, "What have you done to deserve this?" I was ashamed as I walked away home, then... *bang!*

Lilia Gillingham (11)
The Bourne Academy, Bournemouth

IT WASN'T ALWAYS BAD

Just a young boy who was infected by a horrid, rotten creature...

It wasn't always bad. Jack grew up to be carnage in a person. He would murder religiously every night. But revenge is in the air.

There was a scientist who tried to take him out, but it never worked. He caused Jack loads of pain and suffering. Jack was stronger now. Wanting him dead, Jack stormed to the facility, bust open the door and grabbed the scientist. He ripped his head clean off. He didn't have time to scream. But the list of revenge was not over yet!

Amelia Catmull (13)
The Bourne Academy, Bournemouth

BIG SHARK'S TRUE INTENTIONS

Hello, I'm Big Shark. People fear me because of my large teeth and size, but I'm not actually dangerous to humans, they're not even my prey! In fact, *they* are the predators. They keep capturing my prey, hunting down me and my family. So much in fact that we could go extinct. We are really endangered with only 500 of us left. It's scary that the next big shark might not happen due to their hunting. I hate to see sharks suffer. Why does this happen? We are just trying to survive and thrive, and at one point we did...

Tyler Guite (12)
The Bourne Academy, Bournemouth

THE BIG GOOD WOLF

The house was as quiet as a mouse. Suddenly, the dreadful Little Red Riding Hood broke down the door. She walked over to the wolf's rickety ancient bed, climbed in and waited... Meanwhile, in the forest, the wolf was picking flowers for his mum. Once he'd collected a beautiful array of flowers, he began to trek home. The big good wolf arrived at his abode, he suddenly became worried as the door was in pieces on the floor. He cautiously walked in and saw his house in a state. He heard snoring upstairs, he walked up and got a scare!

Leo White (11)
The Bourne Academy, Bournemouth

A WITCH'S MYTH

I never really belonged in this world. I'm a witch, a 'good' witch. My enemy is adored by many, but I'm despised.
"That superhero act was all a lie," my enemy announced. I glared at her, stunned.
"By that you mean...?"
She replied that I had to earn the public's respect, I had to become their superhero. I had to make up for what I'd done. As it turns out, she *was* the villain after all. I couldn't believe that this was her true self, her true nature. Was this the end?

Lauren Wilson (11)
The Bourne Academy, Bournemouth

THE TRUTH ABOUT MOTHER GOTHEL

I never really belonged here. Ever since my parents passed away, I've been scared of death. I was left all alone inside my desolate home. This is why I kidnapped Rapunzel... I just wanted happiness and company. She couldn't find out that I was using her for her beauty and company. It was all fine until a few days ago, on her fifteenth birthday, she came to me, crying and said, "You're not my real mother, are you, Gothel?" How could she possibly have found out? I only wanted to feel young again and have her hair...

Lauren Collinson (12)
The Bourne Academy, Bournemouth

THE MINCE FEARTON PUB

Chris dashed into the pub with a desire to drink. He was pleading for the thirst to depart. As he downed the drinks, he began to suspect that he was being stalked. In the pub, as the night flew by like an aeroplane, he left with fear. Suddenly, Chris collapsed due to how intoxicated he was. He saw rays of light and saw a gloomy dark figure glaring over at him, holding a mince pie. He was so drunk, he couldn't move. Dragging along the rough paving, Chris knew that this was his fate. "Argh!" Chris moaned through the sky...

Lucca Paksoy (11)
The Bourne Academy, Bournemouth

BEHIND THE MASK

She had never really forgotten how everyone looked at her...
"Perfect Snow White!"
Years after years of trying everything to be seen as her
daughter was... It was an endless competition but with one
clear winner. Still to this day, she went green with envy as
she watched Snow's success and beauty. Was the 'evil
queen' just a mask? Was it jealousy in disguise? Her plan to
be on top had failed, but it wasn't yet complete. She would
win. Even if it meant doing something she would soon
deeply regret...

Mia Koumbas (12)
The Bourne Academy, Bournemouth

THE FORGIVEN DEVIL

I started to think that I had done something wrong. I needed to redeem myself after all the wars and battles I'd started. Even though I'm a devil, I can change. I will do this by helping to defeat the Titans in their apocalyptic world. I can take out at least half of the Titans.

It was horrible seeing all of those abandoned houses, land and also decomposed bodies of animals and humans. After finding the first Titan, my soulless wings started to fade into a greyish black. Instead of being a devil, I became a dark angel...

Jean-Paul Nicholls (13)
The Bourne Academy, Bournemouth

RIVALS

I was walking, ready at my spot, glaring down at the city below. My plan was set, ready, in motion. I was then set up, ready to fire, laughing vigorously, still not forgetting what he had done to me and my family. I was then about to shoot, ready for victory and glory. Then suddenly, someone knocked on the door! "How dare they interrupt me!" It was him, my rival's sidekick. Knowing what I was up to he had to go first. *Bang!* I shot him. Blood poured out of his body. Now time for *him*, my biggest rival...

Zach Roach (11)
The Bourne Academy, Bournemouth

HAPPILY EVER AFTER, OR SO YOU THOUGHT...

They thought they got rid of me when I fell down the chimney again. Well, they were wrong and I'm back for revenge.

I walked down the street and saw a very familiar brick house. I filled with anger as I walked closer towards the house. This was the pigs' house; it hadn't changed a bit. I looked up and decided, *I need to get in through there.* My plan was simple: rob the pigs and burn down the house. When I was done, I almost did it, I just didn't see that the old black chimney was smoking violently...

Grace Smith (13)
The Bourne Academy, Bournemouth

IS MEDUSA ALL THAT BAD?

When I was born, I had the worst luck. Everywhere I went, there were disasters: earthquakes, tsunamis and fires. My parents begged the god Zeus to help hide me from the world. I felt betrayed. That's when he gave me the curse. Whoever I laid eyes on instantly turned to stone. It started off with me hearing whispers in my head, people chatting to each other and then *they* started growing. There were snakes on my head. I noticed other changes like my eyes, voice and teeth. How could my parents do this? I seek revenge...

Daisy Bayley-White (12)
The Bourne Academy, Bournemouth

THE FINAL FUNNY CHAT

"Joker!" Batman cries with his heavy suit beating me to the ground. "Why do you do this?" he screams in my face, hitting me again and again.
"Well, you see, Bats, it's all in my backstory. My love cheated with my brother, he had a knife and said, "Why so serious?" and cut me a big smile, so I used the same knife to kill him and his new love, and it felt good. I never wanted to stop!" I explained. "I never fit in and just wanted to fit in. I had a rough childhood..."

William Mbenga (12)
The Bourne Academy, Bournemouth

KING OF DEATH

This is torture. The King of Death has risen. The King of Death has arrived and there are hundreds dead, others hiding and safe. Will others make it out alive? The kingdom wants to know why he's doing this. More are dead, others worrying, not knowing what's going on. He doesn't know what he's doing and asks for forgiveness. They're not accepting. The King of Death gets sad, so they agree.

A while later, he promises not to hurt anyone ever again, so the kingdom and the King of Death become friends.

Keira Skinner (11)
The Bourne Academy, Bournemouth

CINDERELLA AND HER WONDERFUL STEPMUM

I never really belonged. As I walked out of the kitchen, I glanced at Cinderella. As she wiped the tears from her eyes, I could tell that she was distressed. As the day proceeded, I could tell that she was working very hard like she normally does. Cinderella is kind-hearted, always does her best and has a smile on her face no matter what. Sometimes, I hear her sobbing at night since she's lost her father. I do feel bad for her a lot. She thinks that I'm a witch. Deep down, I long to live and be like Cinderella...

Summer Card (12)
The Bourne Academy, Bournemouth

WHAT'S BEHIND THE MASK?

Dear New York,

I'm not who you think I am. It's Batman. He is the true villain here. What you see is what he wants you to see. I'm locked up and he made a hologram of me but made it, you know, look evil. I don't really look like that. You can't trust Batman. He has a plan to act all goody then rule the world. If you don't believe me, I have proof. Tonight, the billboard in Central Park will show a video of Batman being his real self. Don't trust him.

Yours sincerely,

The Joker.

Georgia Moutray (11)
The Bourne Academy, Bournemouth

JOKE ON ME

Hi, I'm the Joker. No one really knows why I'm like what I'm like. Going back thirty years, my dad was pushing me to be so perfect, but I wasn't. I never got A+, only B, which stood for *bad*. As soon as I got home, straight away he would shout and tell me I'm a big disappointment. I always wondered what happened to my runaway mom. I found out my dad had brutally killed my mother.

At age fourteen, I was in a foster home with bad people. So here I am, killing everyone who gets in my way...

Isabelle Preston (12)
The Bourne Academy, Bournemouth

GREGORY

Gregory had been bullied since he attended school because he was born into poverty. It was getting so bad that he moved to the exact school he wanted to go to, but it didn't help because the bullies moved to the same school as Gregory and it got worse. They even started taking his food from his lunchbox, and this made poor little Gregory sad. Every single day, after school, he would sob and sob, trying to think of a way to stop this incessant bullying. Quickly, he thought of one amazing idea. To go on a rampage...

Luke Spinks (12)
The Bourne Academy, Bournemouth

COVID-19 BACKGROUND

Once upon a time, there was a so-called 'villain' named Covid-19. He was born and raised on Jupiter. When he was three years old, another Covid-19 popped up and suddenly the planet (Jupiter) blew up and sent a shockwave launching him to Earth. Then the other to the moon. When he was there, he suddenly saw a human and went in their mouth. He was stuck there for six years till the human died and he blew up into other people. Then he saw a vaccine eating someone's heart. He tried to stop him but he failed...

D'Angelo Mckenzie-Cook (12)
The Bourne Academy, Bournemouth

ALONE

I never belonged. I was neglected by my father when I was born and was left with my mother. My mother passed when I was fourteen. No one in my family would dare take care of me. No one loved me. No one.

Years later, I found out that my uncle tried to save my mother but failed. He was the killer. He said to my face, "No one cares about you and the only one who did is gone forever." I was broken. That's when I wanted revenge.

"I am going to kill you! I'm going to kill everyone."

Jaydn Hardy (13)
The Bourne Academy, Bournemouth

I AM COVID-19

I just wanted some friends. As soon as I came to town, everyone left. They wore these stupid paper things covering their noses and mouths. They shut their doors in my face. They stayed inside for seven months. No one to play with. No one to talk to. No one at all. So I took people with me. People suddenly became furious, depressed and unwelcoming. People tried to keep me away with vaccines and boosters. I never meant to hurt anyone at first, I was lonely. No one ever wanted me around. I just wanted some friends...

Bryonie Cliffe (13)
The Bourne Academy, Bournemouth

I WAS ON MY DAY OFF

I'm having a day off from robberies, and thinking about what to do. I know. Let's go to Paris. I'll rent a helicopter and fly there.

On the way to Paris, I had a moment when I thought I was normal, but reality struck me that no matter how hard I try, I can't change. But I am going to try acting normal for a day. I landed the helicopter, it was amazing and I realised how much I was missing out on. Walking on the street, I saw the shimmering diamonds. Even when I'm normal evil surrounds me!

Natasha Daniels (12)

The Bourne Academy, Bournemouth

THE RIDER

I left the village with a feeling of regret, as if spirits of the dead villagers were watching me flee their burning village. I fled as fast as my horse would go. I rode for hours through the harsh desert. I was dehydrated and in and out of consciousness, wanting to stop, but the thought of the law and spirits made me want to keep going. *Bang...* The law had caught up and put a bullet in the skull of my horse! I ducked behind a boulder, getting out of the line of fire. I peeked over...
Bang!

Rhys Jenkins (14)
The Bourne Academy, Bournemouth

THE RUNNER

I had to make up for what I'd done to them. Do you want to know? Well, it wasn't that pleasant. I threw someone off a bridge into a lava pit, and for the other it was a gruesome fall into an acid pit.

I need to find someone and tell them that I need help.

Ten minutes later, I arrived at my friend's house and he started to make us fake passports to get to Scotland. Eight minutes later, we landed and we had to start running. We ran through streets and alleys. Then suddenly, *boom...!*

Alex Sherring (13)

The Bourne Academy, Bournemouth

RIOT, RULER OF THE GALAXY

I never really belonged in this world, I belonged in my own. I need to rule this galaxy. I'm Riot, ruler of the symbiotes. I've come to this Earth to conquer. I will be the ruler of the galaxy and there is only one person in my way. Venom. I'll find him and fight him like I did in my world that time he escaped from my grasp, but this time I'll catch him off guard. Scattering in panic, losing his head, he'll suffer for the last time. I'll make this world mine, and the galaxy will be mine!

Ben Habgood (11)
The Bourne Academy, Bournemouth

THE SECRET

I've got a secret, nobody knows it. I walk into my dusty old lair and plop myself down on my throne. I must plan my next move. I could rob a bank? Yeah, I'll do that. Hopping off my old chair, I skip over to my cloner. I slam down on the big red button. Wow, do I really look like that? I snap back to reality. I grab my clonermiser. I shoot my clone; it looks different now. I send it to the bank. People swarm out, I enter. Suddenly, I'm being held at gunpoint.
"We know your secret..."

Tayler Rees (13)
The Bourne Academy, Bournemouth

THE CIRCUS IN THE MIDDLE OF THE WOODS

I still haven't forgotten when I was made fun of because I was a clown with a throwing knife and threw it at everyone. I killed. I put an alive doll in their pack. Now I live in the middle of the woods, in the circus tent, as a skeleton clown. Life is a misery. But every so often, many people come in and get scared and run away because they remember my story... Speaking of it... here someone comes along now. I'm going to go down from the top of the tent and greet them. "Hello there," I say...

Jack Smith (12)
The Bourne Academy, Bournemouth

TRUE FREEDOM

I did it to survive my evil overlord. If I didn't listen, I would've been killed; I could've been replaced in seconds. My task was to kill Cyro, some hero causing us trouble. I set off to find him and a few hours later we were face-to-face. He gave up a fight, but I was victorious in the end, my superior equipment shining through. However, on the way back, I felt a pang of guilt. Was this really a victory? Serving an evil villain with no other purpose? No. I will find a way to escape. I promise...

Lucas Bushnell (12)

The Bourne Academy, Bournemouth

KILLER?

One year. Five months. Two weeks. One day. I have been stuck in this jail cell. Everyone calls me evil, a villain, a killer. Am I a villain? Maybe I am, but what about the good things I've done? Do they not count? I helped *them* with crops, buildings, war. But I guess they don't remember the good old days before they turned on me. I had my own team with George, Mark and Hannah. I bet they are glad that I'm rotting in here. They all turned on me, so I had to kill them. Did they deserve it?

Jasmin Morris (13)
The Bourne Academy, Bournemouth

THE TRUTH BEHIND THE T-REX!

I was trying to amuse myself by spinning around when, all of a sudden, I heard screaming. Looking down, I saw small children traumatised! Three velociraptors were snapping at them. My hands were too short to pick them up, so I had to use my mouth. Then, *bang!* I swallowed them. It wasn't my fault! They created the beast in me. I never meant to hurt them. I destroyed their one precious life. I didn't mean to. It was all a misunderstanding. I need to make up for what I have done. Why... Why me?

Olivia Chilcott (12)
The Bourne Academy, Bournemouth

THE NOT-SO-BAD WOLF?

I never really belonged when I was growing up. People were always scared of me, so I hid away in the deep dark woods, away from people. It was peaceful in there away from civilisation. Until one day, a little girl with a red hood skipped through the woods with a basket full of snacks like cookies and other delicious things. I asked if I could have one, but she said, "No!" and hit me with her basket. So I used self-defence as she really hurt me. The next thing I know, I am known as the big bad wolf?

William Colegate (12)
The Bourne Academy, Bournemouth

LET ME BE FREE

I never really belonged in my family. Both my parents were villains, and looking back, I never wanted to be that. I always got picked to be the bad guy and never nice. When I finally got to be nice, I realised that I didn't want to be like my parents. I still haven't forgotten when I mocked people, and every time I wanted to throw my rubbish in the bin, my parents made me put it on the floor. My parents made me do their dirty work because an innocent child couldn't do such things. Let me be free!

Neve Sewell (11)
The Bourne Academy, Bournemouth

THE WATERFALL

I grabbed the wedding dress bag and dragged it to the end of the mountain. I gave a sigh of relief. I will never forget what that person did to me. The anger was boiling in my blood as I thought of the humiliation that I experienced that month. This is my perfect victory to clear my name; nothing could go wrong now.

A branch snapped, making shivers run down my spine. I glanced over and glanced back. As I pulled the zip, my heart stopped - where was she? I felt a cold hand on my back. I fell forwards...

Emily Hall (13)
The Bourne Academy, Bournemouth

VOLDEMORT THE VILLAIN?

I never really belonged. I was always being bullied. More than anyone. Lily and James Potter were the worst of them all. They blackmailed me, they framed me, they threatened me. The superhero act was a lie. They were evil. I was alone, no one to talk to. I just wanted power. I felt like the world was caving in on me. I was pressured into turning evil. Everyone would disown me. I needed an escape route. That night I attacked them, all of the bad memories came flooding in, drowning me. I had to do it.

Evie Clark (12)
The Bourne Academy, Bournemouth

THE TRUTH COMES OUT!

The superhero act was all a lie... Snow White was never your hero. I was! The evil queen. I found out one evening who she really was. Like always, I brought the king his tea and all of a sudden, *splat!* I walked in... The ruby-red blood was all over the walls. She looked at me, *bang!* I dropped the tea! The blood was dripping off the knife. I knew, at this moment, I needed to take matters into my own hands. Little did I know, she blamed it all on me. I tried to protect this kingdom!

Amber Spillane (12)
The Bourne Academy, Bournemouth

ALL I WANTED WAS SOME COMPANY...

I never thought that this day would come... My dearest child, Rapunzel, found out that I was using her for my own sake and beauty. I was never able to have my own child/company, so when I saw her beauty, I decided to make her mine. One night (when she was two), I was brushing her hair and I felt a little... dazed. I'm not sure how to explain it, but for the first time in ages I felt young again. That was because I *was* young again... After I found this out, I hid her away for myself...

Lillie Kohon

The Bourne Academy, Bournemouth

THE SOUL EATER

I did it to survive. My powers were weak. Voices banged in my head, trying to break free. My mind was being set free, my body failing and dying on me. My vision was fading away. I was about five metres away from the souls locked away in my black diamond cauldron.

I was now about one metre from the cauldron. I could not see now. Finally, I could feel the cauldron in my damp hands. I unlocked it. Launched my hand into the cauldron. My vision was back. To this day, I still want my revenge...

Max Perkins (14)
The Bourne Academy, Bournemouth

THE HEARTBROKEN MERMAID

I can hear her, Ariel. If only she knew what her father did. The fool broke my heart and cursed me to be a hybrid. It started with me being human, him falling for me and making me like him. I fell for him too until he left me for another. He chose her and cursed me. He loved my voice, so that's why I'm going to take it from his daughter. I wasn't always like this; he made me like this. I went from loving and warm to mean and cold. I'll have my revenge; I'll make him pay!

Luana Da Cruz (12)
The Bourne Academy, Bournemouth

THE KILLER BAT

The superhero act was a lie. He was an evil man, but no one believed me. Batman was his name. It started when he and I were younger. We despised each other. He bullied me. It got so bad that I had to do something. I grew up wanting to get him back, but he disappeared. No one had seen him. Until I was walking with my daughter when we heard gunshots. Sadly, she was caught in the crossfire. I saw a glimpse of the man who shot the gun. Batman killed my daughter. I chased him down the alley...

Tilly Westcott (12)
The Bourne Academy, Bournemouth

BITTER BEAUTY OF BLOOD

Greetings. I am an undead entity. It is in your instincts to fear me; no matter though, I have no interest in thy lamentable nature to be panic-stricken. But do not coil; I wish thou no harm. I wasn't always a vile, bloodthirsty monstrosity. I had a wealthy family and wonderful living quarters. I was due to complete my betrothed marriage and claim my title as dame, but it was stolen from me... as bloodshed was all around me, leaving me to rot in my new unyielding form. Alone forever.

Skye Goldsack (14)
The Bourne Academy, Bournemouth

THE BACKSTORY OF MALEFICENT

Maleficent was not always bad. When she was a child, she was the fairest in the land. She had golden hair that went to her shoulders, but her mum was horrid to her, cutting her wrist until she went pale. She ran away one day until she came to a cliff's edge. She ran off it. Then a flash of black covered her body. She had so much evil in her life that she became bad. She grew wings after a week and then the world felt like it was in her disgusting, evil, horrid hands. She was evil...

Chloe Calvert (12)

The Bourne Academy, Bournemouth

TRICK OR TREAT?

Bang! The door slammed against the old creepy wood. "The last Halloween was bad, but this one is going to be the one. I know it is." He grabbed his mask ready for tonight. Someone's doorbell rang, they thought it was the trick-or-treaters, but it was someone else. "Who are you?" the man said.

"Your worst nightmare." *Stab!* There was silence. Nothing else was heard. The blood came pouring out. Next stop, the police station...

Charlie Cherrett (12)
The Bourne Academy, Bournemouth

SHARK BAIT

I was swimming around the deep part of the ocean, searching for food until I saw a boat. When I was young, I always got told not to go near boats since they would always proceed to give a bad response. This time, I took a risk. But then I got distracted. A long wire with food... I've been searching for ages. I started to move without swimming. The boat was moving fast. The only thing I could do was hit it. Maybe I hit it too hard since it took me somewhere deadly (the engine)...

Harry Owen (12)
The Bourne Academy, Bournemouth

THE INNOCENT 'VILLAIN'

When I was younger, my mother badly abused me, so I ran away from home at the age of ten and villains raised me from ten to fifteen, then let me go off on a hunt to find my mother. I went to the house and no one was there. "Where is she?" I asked myself. Someone knew I was going there; it was my auntie, she told me that my mother was dead. I was devastated because I didn't want to kill her, I just wanted to say hi.

I went and killed myself too. This ends with me.

Phoebe Palmer (12)

The Bourne Academy, Bournemouth

THE BOY WITH NO FRIENDS

Many families come and go from this house. Sometimes because rent is too high or they don't like the area, but the main reason for this is because of Toby. A young ghost boy who will never make a friend. The reason for this is that before his death he was cursed, so anytime a young child sees him, they go through weeks of pain that lead to death. He never meant for any of this to ever happen. He is too young to know what he is doing, but he is always seen as the villain...

Bella Manton-Kelly (12)
The Bourne Academy, Bournemouth

MS TRUNCHBULL: BEHIND THE SCENES

My name is Ms Trunchbull and I actually love children. I hated the fact that I had to put children in the Chokey. That was just to scare them and make them better children. I used to work in a shop, but changing to a school was the best decision. To be fair, most people now call me the best principal and the best person in the world that they have ever met. I love playing games, oh and you know that cat? He loves me so much. I didn't want to kick the cat, but I had to...

Brooklyn Cliffe (11)
The Bourne Academy, Bournemouth

CHOICES

Whip! Pow! Bang! Holding the power of my foe right in my hand, his blood-drooling face stared off at the sight of my new city. I felt invincible. Untouched. But something changed. I stared into his unconscious eyes, realising something. I'm not sure what it was, but now I was in shock. From all of the things I've done in my life; all the evil. My eyes shrank as if I was a failure. Of nothing but the thrill of being a criminal. I've won, but at what cost?

Connor Foy (13)
The Bourne Academy, Bournemouth

POISON DART MAYHEM

Doctor Dart walked down the path suspiciously and acknowledged everything. He was trying to find out who was poisoning the town's food with poison dart frog poison. He was joined by Sir Freda - a poison dart frog. Everyone was suspicious of him. Suddenly, Dr Dart's walkie-talkie went off.

"You're out of time."

So they had to guess. Naturally, since they had no information, they went for Freda. But they were wrong. It was Dr Dart all along...

Quinn Humphreys (12)

The Bourne Academy, Bournemouth

BELONGING

I never really belonged. I was always bullied, my family hated me. That's why I did what I did. I'm not a bad person, but my family were. I always tried to fit in, but that was a big mistake! That was it. I got my long black coat and ran away. I was fed up with all the glares and whispers I got when I walked down the street. If only they knew the truth. So I moved to a new little town far from home, hoping that the people from the town didn't know my history...

Scarlett King (12)
The Bourne Academy, Bournemouth

LURKING IN THE SHADOWS

There was a boy, a boy who sought peace - peace for the world, by disposing of the world's evil. A crime-free world; wouldn't that be great? Or so he thought. After he discovered he had the ability to time travel, he began to dispose of anybody who dared to commit a crime. Finally, he had achieved what he wanted, but instead of a crime-free world, it became a fear-filled one. A feared atmosphere where the mass killer was lurking in the shadows, waiting for them...

K Green (14)

The Bourne Academy, Bournemouth

WHY DOES EVERYONE HATE ME?

There I was, born, but why so early? The day after I entered the world, a human chased me and I tried to run away until I was picked up and taken to their house! They let me go the next day, but my family wouldn't let me back. What did I do? I arrived back, but nobody wanted me! I got upset. I had no family.

It changed me forever and from that day I swore to not let anyone touch me again, never let them get close - close enough to hurt. Why did it have to be me?

Olivia Martin (13)

The Bourne Academy, Bournemouth

THE DOLL'S PAST

When I was younger, all I wanted was to be loved. Yet all my family ignored me and were always too busy with work. I had a doll that was my only friend. I would always pretend that she was a real person. Every night, I would put her on a chair next to my bed. But one night, when I was perfectly asleep, someone had left the oven on and a fire started. My parents got out of the house, yet they had left me in the house! I died that night. My soul got trapped in the doll...

Alicia Washington (11)
The Bourne Academy, Bournemouth

BALLET TRAUMA

I never really belonged doing ballet. I never found it entertaining, nor fun. One time, I couldn't attend my ballet lesson because I felt ill - my mother decided to mistreat me because of it. I told my mother that it left my feet bleeding and made me insecure about my figure. Mother then suddenly had enough of my complaining and Mother decided to sew the pointe shoes to my feet. Needles, thread and blood all over the floor. They're still with me to this day.

Esmé Collins (11)
The Bourne Academy, Bournemouth

SUPER WICKED WOLF

I never really belonged in a world like this. I'm vicious and I don't know how to change. I'm powerful, tall and strong. One little old lady ruined my life when she burned my whole family in a haystack. I will not rest until I'm avenged. Red Riding Hood is always taking selfies in the woods, she thinks that she's all that! Well, I know that her grandma is evil, so I'm going to save her from such a wicked woman and wait for her to thank me...

Liam Spiers (12)
The Bourne Academy, Bournemouth

ALONE WITH EVIL

I don't remember much after my mum passed away. All I remember is that I have lived with my dad since I was three. Living with Dad has made me who I am. I want to be just like my dad. Like his evilness. In order to do that, I have to do something mega evil. So I decided to sink a boat. What I did was I snuck behind the captain and killed him so then I could take over the boat and trap people in a room. Then the boat was never seen again. *Dun, dun, dun!*

Keryn Turner-Dodd (12)
The Bourne Academy, Bournemouth

THE UNMISTAKABLE FIGURE

I never really belonged as I was an A* kind of student, but one day everything changed... I was getting followed home by a group of boys. One of them put their hand near my face to punch me, so I pulled my hands out of my pockets and, with the power I had to stop them, they were like ashes. I laughed my evil laugh and I pictured the horrible time they were going to have with me in Hell.

Hello, my name is Satan. If you didn't know me before, now you do!

Millie Hansford (12)
The Bourne Academy, Bournemouth

IN THE MIND OF THE HELLHOUND CERBERUS

I never belonged here, in a cage or an arena. They stole me from my home and owner and trapped me here. I knew I had to make up for my mistake - but not like this! Why, of all the things they could've done, did they do this? They shackled me down, left me to die, laughed at me time after time and then beat me with brutal weapons and chariots. Now my plan is in motion. I will run away tonight, escape this murderous pit. Now for the hard part...

Tom Craig (12)
The Bourne Academy, Bournemouth

TALE OF MUZA

My life has been one of much shame. When I was born, I barely had a pulse and the doctors said I wouldn't live past twenty. When I was twenty, I was on my deathbed. They gave me a new medicine called Spider Lily. It barely had an effect and killed the doctor in a rage! But there *was* a change. The sun almost killed me so I can't go outside. Since I am a demon, I made a group called Upper Moans. There were seven to protect me...

Daniel Hall (12)

The Bourne Academy, Bournemouth

THE THREE BEARS

I was having a day off with the family, but it got bad. Our door was open, there was an intruder. Our food was missing, our chairs were broken. We found a young blonde girl in bed, so we tied her up. We were curious. She had a crowbar. We called the cops, but our animal instincts came over us. We killed the intruder before realising what we had done. We were in shock. We were murderers. We blamed it on our neighbours...

William Rendell (12)
The Bourne Academy, Bournemouth

SO MUCH FOR MY DAY OFF

I'm having a day off from being a villain. I went to the joke shop to get some more epic tricks. Then I went to the circus, then I shouted at the clown that I was more hilarious than him. It was hilarious and made me feel amazing. After that, I went and got my hair done and my face repainted. I was looking fabulous! I ruined it all by getting into an argument with a bus driver. He's dead now. So much for a day off!

Kieran Dominey-Patterson (13)
The Bourne Academy, Bournemouth

AFTER EVER AFTER

I still haven't forgotten that this villain costume is all fake. "I do have a nose, and Harry Potter doesn't!" He's got my nose. The little thief. I'm going to get revenge. I am going to find him.
I opened my door and went. "Why's everyone looking at me?" I looked down and my costume... I wasn't wearing my costume. The truth was revealed.

Jorja Spiers (11)
The Bourne Academy, Bournemouth

RED RIDING HOOD TURNS BAD!

I never really belonged anywhere. I had no friends, nobody to trust. My mum and dad never ever had time for me. They only had time for my fifteen brothers and sisters. I felt like I was an outcast. So I decided to make a plan. I had this idea in my head that if I poisoned them, I would be the favourite child.

One night, I told my mother that I would make dinner for all of them...

Honey-Mae White (12)

The Bourne Academy, Bournemouth

DRACO

My plan was to try and get the one and only Harry Potter. Every time I try, Hagrid comes and stops me. It's always Hagrid or Voldemort. They might do something. I really need to kill him and after I get him, *if* I get him, I will try and kill everyone else in Hogwarts like Hermione Granger and Ron Weasley. I hope Voldemort will be proud of me and my dad...

Ellie Ashby (12)
The Bourne Academy, Bournemouth

THE TRUTH BEHIND MYSTERIO

My name is Mysterio. I come from Planet Y19. I'm the last of my kind. I had to fight for my planet against Titans bigger than I've ever seen. They were known as the Elementals. And now I'm here in search of the final four Elementals: Earth, Fire, Wind and Water. I'm now looking for someone strong enough to help me on my journey...

Layton Murrell (12)
The Bourne Academy, Bournemouth

THE SORRY VILLAIN

I had to make up for what I had done. It was my day off, so I went out for the day. Suddenly, everyone hid from me because they thought that I would do something bad to their pretty and colourful city.
"I need to quickly show people that I am not evil and that I was made to do it," I said to myself...

Stacey Moore-Nichols (12)
The Bourne Academy, Bournemouth

BELONGING

I never really belonged anywhere. Countless homes; rejected. All of my memories are altered, apart from one. Bruce Wayne chasing me with a gun.

Pew! The bullet had grazed the side of my cheek. Ever since then, the Joker and I have been trying to take my revenge and finally escape my past...

Archie Carrigan (12)

The Bourne Academy, Bournemouth

SHREK'S DAY OFF

I'm having a day off from being Shrek. Today, I'm going to a five-star swamp to relax.
When I arrive, I try and settle down and sleep, but I hear the unforgettable sound of a neigh. There is a donkey here. I never get a day off!

Elijah Pestell (11)
The Bourne Academy, Bournemouth

THE TIME HAS ARRIVED

A god between mortal men. That's what I desire to be. That's what the cauldron can make me. But how do I maintain the cauldron? How will I get it in my grasp? A god between mortal men. That's what rewinds my patience back. The thought of having that title.

My men went silent. Too silent. My dragons stopped roaring. That's when I escaped my thoughts. My thoughts of becoming a god between mortal men. Flames erupted, blanketing the tables and flags. Men fled. My dragons broke their chains. All I did was grip onto my throne. But the cauldron...

Ocean Melody Jackson (12)
The Littlehampton Academy, Littlehampton

AVENGE US

Everyone believes that villains are just plain evil, but no one knows what happens to turn us evil. Are we evil or are we the heroes in disguise? Stories are always told from the hero's point of view. Are they the villains of the stories? Is Captain Hook the villain or is Peter Pan? The information you get shows that Peter Pan is the hero, but what if Captain Hook was trying to release the Lost Boys? Stories from different points of view change our opinions. We, as villains, need to have our story told. They need the whole truth.

Philippa Jordan-Watts (14)

The Littlehampton Academy, Littlehampton

DEEP INTO MY SOUL

I wake up in a jail cell, the walls crumbly with mouldy bricks, matt black-like paint. I look down at my clothing. I realise that I'm wearing a bright orange jumpsuit with a badge that says '001'. That is when I realise that I am in a jail cell in Arksham Asylum. I hold the rusty iron bars when I scream in pain. I find a sharp stone on the floor and start carving out an escape plan. As I clean my face in the rusty sink, I stare into the mirror and I'm staring deep into my soul...

Archie Childs
The Littlehampton Academy, Littlehampton

MISS TRUNCHBULL'S REVENGE

I still haven't forgotten when Miss Trunchbull put us all in the Chokey.

Miss Trunchbull walked in... "Good afternoon children!"

"Good afternoon Miss Trunchbull."

The class stared at the head teacher. She stared back...

"Today I am your teacher."

Matilda and her classmates weren't happy.

"How do you spell 'newt'?" she yelled.

Eric stood up. "Erm, N... E... W... T."

"Wrong! I said mute! To the Chokey, ha!"

Break time... The class ran out as quick as they could.

"Get back here... *now!* Chokey, Chokey, Chokey! Now go before I ring your parents!"

Will Miss Trunchbull ever get caught out?

Lucy Marshall (11)
Unsworth Academy, Bury

BLACK

I still haven't forgotten. Ten years prior, Andromida kicked out of the family. Father forcing me into marriage. Black wild hair whipping in the wind. My bright green eyes shone like stars in the sky. I could hear the voice of Rodolfus in my ear whispering, "He can set you free, he can give you a way out."

"Bellatrix, have you found a rich Pureblood wizard to marry yet?" yelled out her mother.

"Bella, join us." There it was again. Rodolfus' voice ringing through my head. "You want freedom? He can give it to you." So I joined him. Voldemort.

Sophie Wood (13)
Unsworth Academy, Bury

THE TWELVE-YEAR-OLD MONSTER

"Night, Ma." Tanner closed his innocent eyes, but when he did, he was no longer himself. The thermal vision could tell the difference between human flesh and the dead meat of one of his victims. He would always wake up and think about his 'dream', but this night was different. He began to feel like his violent dream was lasting ages. As he slashed the throat of an unlucky victim, he saw a 'missing' poster. Tanner, twelve years old. It was him. His villainous grin turned into a horrifying, green, spotty, goblin-like frown. He's evil. He's a monster. Argh! Murder!

Sam Krelle (13)
Unsworth Academy, Bury

THE DIARY OF THE VILLAINOUS MR WASP

Dear Diary,

The weekend is here, so here's a catch-up. Monday, I stole some honey from the bees, but Mr Security Guard gave me a bruise.

Tuesday, I took the children to the playground but the swings were monumental.

Wednesday, a mid-week fish and chips snack, but I lost Gary when a cup went on him.

Thursday was a night with the Mrs, although brother Jerry was in an awful state with the kids.

Friday, watched a bit of AntsBob RoundPants.

For the weekend, not much is planned other than being with the family. Goodbye, from Mr Wasp the Villainous.

Barney Williams (12)
Unsworth Academy, Bury

'CEREAL' KILLER

Bang! Bang! Bang!
"Die, die!" the 'cereal' killer yelled as he plunged his knife into his victim. The sound of banging and crashing shook the house. Cereal was everywhere that the eye could see. He had killed his sixth victim. His victim was as well known as choco pops. Now he must plan his next murder. It was going to be Chocolate Pillows. His reason: they are too sweet with little chocolate inside. He will do it tomorrow at 12:30am. He will be alone at home. He will kill his victim quietly and with little mess. He'll use a surprise...

Charlie Shearn
Unsworth Academy, Bury

LAST KIDS ON EARTH

Landon and his friends were trying to fill the Beastiary, but what they didn't know was that Kloner was using that book to bring Resock to Earth! They then fought the water-monster. Landon, Jack, June and Durk officially completed the Beastiary and gave it back to Kloner. That very same night, they went into the forest only to come across Kloner chanting to the tree. At that very moment, they knew what he needed the Beastiary for... To bring Resock to Earth. They had to stop him before it was too late. Landon eventually killed Kloner, but not Resock...!

India Wilson (11)
Unsworth Academy, Bury

MISUNDERSTOOD

When we're younger, we're told the stories of good and bad, light and dark, heroes and villains. What we're not told is that not everyone falls into those categories. There are people in-between. The reason no one talks about those people is that no one really knows what to call us. Are we good? Bad? Misunderstood? No one knows. In a perfect world, all those questions would be answered and we'd all be fine. But this isn't a perfect world and there's no way to escape it either. I should know. I have spent my whole life trying to.

Sophie Turrell-Kinsella (13)
Unsworth Academy, Bury

WHY AM I THE 'WICKED' ONE?

Cinderella was my third daughter, she was naive and clumsy. As a mother, I was scared for her. However, that wasn't the only reason I kept her away. My first husband, Baron of Meldavia, gave me two beautiful daughters but not everyone thought so. Hence, when I met Cinderella, I realised my children would not have a chance with her elegant looks. I decided to keep her out of the spotlight until my children got courted. Tears trickled down her face as she realise that she failed, as she looked glumly upon the white letter stamped with the royal seal.

Ayshe Smith (13)
Unsworth Academy, Bury

137

RED DRESS

I still always remember the crash so vividly. it still haunts me to this day. My friend died that night. She was wearing that white floral dress she always loved and wore. At school, she was popular. Always kept up with the latest trends.
Everyone adored her. She would always pick on me to make herself look better. It worked, obviously. She would always leave me in the dark and act like I wasn't there. She caused me so much pain, but I stayed with her.
I'm not sorry for causing the crash. Her dress looked better stained red anyway...

Grace Landsborough (13)
Unsworth Academy, Bury

I WASN'T REALLY EVIL

She needed to learn a lesson. She had everything that she wanted. *Spoilt.* So I taught her a lesson. I made her cook, made her clean. I made her do *everything*. It was fair. She deserved it for how spoilt she was. She disobeyed me. She went to the ball. She shouldn't have gone to the ball. She deserved everything that she got. I hate her. She needed to be taught a lesson. What I did wasn't *evil*; it was fair. It was deserved. She's evil. Not me. Blame her. Not me. What you think I did wasn't really evil.

Thomas Dawes (12)
Unsworth Academy, Bury

THE DEVOURING

The Earth shook as lava burst through the ground. Its raging waves consumed the newly built houses. The fortune teller was right; we *are* food. Screaming pierced my ears as the Earth's crust started to split. Jagged jaws formed and thousands of people fell into the never-ending crater. Sea water and clouds combined to make two devious-looking eyes. Trees fell. We were doomed. A thought went across his mind as he gave up and drifted to a better place. Everyone was gone. These events rarely happened. It was time for all to restart...

Elias Spencer (13)
Unsworth Academy, Bury

ROBOTIC

I have never really belonged. I am not human but something else. I'm sent on assassinations. I have never failed. I was sent to kill two parents and... a child. It was the king. I climbed twenty storeys and shattered the window. My eyes glowing red with the instinct to kill. I was shot, hit, but nothing could pierce my metal body. I charged through their defence, killing everyone in my path. The mother shot me, so I executed the king. I sliced my hand through his skin and, gasping for air, I dropped him. The vengeful daughter escaped...

Oliver Abouna-Matthews (13)
Unsworth Academy, Bury

THE MYSTERY OF THE VAMPIRE

I still remember that day when a young girl in all black was sat on top of a car roof. As I walked towards her, I asked if she was alright although she stayed silent. I began to walk again, suddenly it lashed down with rain and thunder. I heard an evil laugh behind me. I looked over my shoulder, there was the girl. The car was burning. She smiled and lowered her head, showing her teeth which had blood dripping from them in her mouth. I stuttered and couldn't speak. She said, "You're next, my friend," and took me...

Summer Makin (13)
Unsworth Academy, Bury

I'M INNOCENT

I'm innocent. I never meant to kill anyone. I was trying to stop him from finishing it; I couldn't let him publish it. I needed money to fund my next book. If he published it, I wouldn't be able to appeal anything. It's not my fault; he shouldn't have been there. I knew it. I knew what he should do, but he didn't. He should have left. The fire wasn't meant to spread, it was just meant to burn the building. My book was going to be better anyway, so it doesn't matter. He was a goner. I am innocent.

Thomas Dunphy (13)
Unsworth Academy, Bury

DESTRUCTION

Mr Loftus is a teacher who hates children. He came into possession of a nuclear suitcase bomb. He planned to set the bomb off when he was far away from the school. Soon, everyone would die. He grinned maniacally as he set the timer for one hour. He would 'leave to get food' and never return. Not that there would be anything to return to. He would escape the country and his lonely life forever. He left the school for the last time. When he arrived home, he turned on the news to see the destruction that he would cause...

Jake Rosie (13)

Unsworth Academy, Bury

THE CURSE OF ED SHEERAN

The Word Bin slouched down on his chair and bought a good chippy from Chippie Shop. "I am going to have a day off." He munched on his chips and tap-danced in the living room whilst listening to the Peppa Pig theme song. He got dressed and went outside to get some cookies at Aldi. He went on his roller skates and rolled down the aisles. "Whee!" A chav stood before him and sang Ed Sheeran. The Word Bin got mad and threw a chocolate bar at her! He started dancing again and went home. What a lovely day today.

Leah Wilson (11)
Unsworth Academy, Bury

OPPOSITE LOCKDOWN

Michael was tired of being unable to leave his room. He knew that it was unfair. He stayed in his room and made tools out of old mechanics. Before the raid, Evil Ian was always watching. From this, he invented the jackhammer. He saw below the ground and realised that he was living on a floating island! The monster Ian's army did not expect Michael to fall down. Wires connected, which made the island. He was free and needed a way to get all the humans off the island. He cut the wire, meaning Ian fell to his death. Free.

Chloé Hill (12)
Unsworth Academy, Bury

SNAPE'S REVENGE

It was all a lie. I faked it all. I never died and was never in love with Harry's mother. I just said that so that he would trust me. Once Dumbledore died, my plan started. I was going to make Voldemort the headmaster. When I ruled the school, I knew that it was going to work. When Dumbledore died, seeing Harry so sad made me so happy; everyone thinks he's so perfect. They've not seen the other side of him, that two-faced boy! His story is over and mine has just begun. Everyone will see that it's not over!

Laila Kirkley (12)
Unsworth Academy, Bury

GOLDILOCKS AND HER SWEET REVENGE

After a couple of weeks of planning, it's time for Goldilocks' revenge. She headed out to the woods and set a trap. Then she screamed. She pretended to be injured so the bears would come and help her, but little did they know, it was a trap. As she suspected, the bears started frantically looking for the girl. They spotted her from a distance. As they ran to her, the baby bear stood on a button. It activated the trap and the cage fell on top of them. They were trapped. They tried to break free but couldn't...

Willow Carter (12)
Unsworth Academy, Bury

THE POWER OF THE HEART

In the land of Forza, a wizard roams the land, using the art of black magic. The wizard split his heart into multiple pieces, creating four monsters at four different corners of the island. The king, Midas, chose a knight to use 'the power of the heart' from the monster equipped with a heart sword to absorb the power of the hearts. First, he got the fire heart from the dragon. After that, he got each heart one by one. He went to fight the wizard, but he was gone. He read the origin one more time, then he died...

Mitchel Massey (13)
Unsworth Academy, Bury

MUM? DAD? I NEED YOU

"I love you," was the last thing he said to me. Although it was all a lie. My name is Emily and I am fourteen years old. Sadly, I'm homeless, living on the street with my mum, and this is my life. My dad left us both when I was nine, with no money to pay the bills or rent. We get at least £10 from those walking by, but that's not enough to pay for everyday essentials.

Three weeks ago, my mum found out that she was diagnosed with cancer, and she needs surgery but we haven't any money...

Brooke Orzel (12)
Unsworth Academy, Bury

REVENGE OF THE ONION

100 years ago, in a land far, far away, lived a princess in a castle. But guarding her tower was a vicious fire-breathing dragon. However, one day, two young things came along to save the princess and awaken her from her slumber. As they got close to the wooden rickety bridge, they noticed the pit of lava below them and fear struck them in the face.
Ten minutes later, they crossed the bridge, snuck in suspicious and awoke the princess. Now the princess was in shock because she was saved by an ogre and a donkey!

Sebastian Brickles (11)
Unsworth Academy, Bury

GRIFFINS AND GARGOYLES

As Fred, Betty, Ali and George entered the room for their punishment, they found a note. It read: 'Play the game and no one will be hurt. From the Griffins and Gargoyles'. That evening, they were all thinking the same thing. So the next day, they started playing. They each had suspicions about who to trust and who not to. They went through a series of tasks like spinning the bottle for your fate. The final task was 'never have I ever'. All their secrets would be uncovered, even the darkest ones...

Scarlett Hunter (11)

Unsworth Academy, Bury

CHUCK PIGEON

I never really belonged. I was always picked on for wanting to be just like Superman, but that's all in my past. I used to go by the name Chuck, now I'm Chuck Pigeon. Now nobody will make fun of me and I will be victorious. Nobody will get in my way. Now I am going to kill everybody who ever doubted me. I will rule the world for eternity. I'll be on the front page, in the news. My name will be known on billboards, in books, stories, gossip. I will be everywhere. I will be known for eternity.

Charlie Howard (12)
Unsworth Academy, Bury

LOFTUS THE CORONA SPREADER

Dr Loftus went to China undercover in the Chinese tradition. He went there to go on a mission to bring Corona to the UK. He spent months and months of planning and it went perfect. He quickly came to the UK with Corona, he injected himself with a needle that took the Corona out of him and into the spreader of truth, who injected everyone with it as soon as they were asleep. They all woke up with Corona and now the UK is full of disease. Now Dr Loftus would sit and watch everyone suffer for eternity.

Dion Senior (14)
Unsworth Academy, Bury

DEATH'S DAY OFF

Today, I woke up and felt good. I've never felt like this because I am, well, Death. I kinda liked it. I thought I would... be good. So I cut up my bedsheets and created a white hood. I have never really liked the colour white, but I might have to change my mind. I now, to this day, feel fabulous. I think that having that day off has changed my point of view. I now show my face around town. I feel like a real human. But even though I try to gossip, I don't think that they're listening...

Will Carter (12)
Unsworth Academy, Bury

THE FINAL WISH

I never really belonged. I was an outcast, the person everyone hated. Until I had had enough. One night, I lay under the stars and wished for everyone to know and fear me. When I woke up, I awoke in a peculiar room with blood splattered on the wall and a body whose face was as white as snow. I wanted to go and check if they were alright, but I couldn't move. I had no control over my body. When I was about to start crying, I spotted a dark figure in the corner of the room.
Silence. Death...

Molly Akturan (13)
Unsworth Academy, Bury

MASON AND THE VILLAIN

It was a nice sunny day. I was listening to the news, it said that a villain had robbed a shop. He looked tall and he robbed a painting of Queen Elizabeth. His name was Mason. My brother!

He came at midnight. He said that he was going to rob my house! So I said that I was going to protect my house. Then he came into my house, so I started kicking and punching him. He said that he was going to take my jewellery and my dog. He was going to take my PlayStation. Then he took them...

Jack Corbett (12)
Unsworth Academy, Bury

THE CAT AND THE BIRDS

The cat - called Jerry - goes outside one day and finds a bird's nest in a tree. The cat decides to climb the tree and get the bird in the nest, but the tree has no way to get up apart from a little branch. So the cat goes for it and jumps up it. When he gets to the top where the nest is, the cat picks up the first bird but it flies away. So the cat goes for the second bird, but it flies away. Then the other birds come and push him out of the tall tree.

Ollie Harris (12)
Unsworth Academy, Bury

CLICK

I still haven't forgotten when I clicked my fingers and the world ended. I have regrets about ending the world. Now I am stuck with no one. I don't know what to do. I am bored. All I have is a book and a pencil and a rubber. People thought that I was a loser, but now I am the king of the world and now I can run the world because no one is here. Now I can live as long as I want. I will rule the world and eat my very own chocolate made by me!

Amy Robinson (12)
Unsworth Academy, Bury

TAKE BACK WHAT ONCE WAS MINE

Yes, I know it was wrong, but I did it to survive. I needed her hair to stay young. I really did care for and love her though. Rapunzel was the sweetest. I haven't forgotten her smile, laugh and how she always wanted me to brush her hair whilst she sang. Sometimes I can still hear her singing when I'm alone, but she hates me now and I can't see her anymore...

Amelia Sherratt (12)
Unsworth Academy, Bury

![YoungWriters Est. 1991]

YOUNG WRITERS INFORMATION

We hope you have enjoyed reading this book – and that you will continue to in the coming years.

If you're a young writer who enjoys reading and creative writing, or the parent of an enthusiastic poet or story writer, do visit our website **www.youngwriters.co.uk**. Here you will find free competitions, workshops and games, as well as recommended reads, a poetry glossary and our blog. There's lots to keep budding writers motivated to write!

If you would like to order further copies of this book, or any of our other titles, then please give us a call or order via your online account.

Young Writers
Remus House
Coltsfoot Drive
Peterborough
PE2 9BF
(01733) 890066
info@youngwriters.co.uk

Join in the conversation!
Tips, news, giveaways and much more!

 **YoungWritersUK** 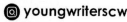 **YoungWritersCW** @ **youngwriterscw**